To Our
Five Little Monkeys

"Balloons!" says Mimi.
"Which one would you like?" asks Papi.
"I want the Monkey Balloon, Papi!"

"Let's take the Monkey Balloon for a walk," says Papi.

"Uh-oh, my Monkey Balloon!" says Mimi.

"Where do you think the Monkey Balloon went?" asks Papi.

"Maybe the Monkey Balloon is eating ice cream
at the ice-cream shop!" says Mimi.

"No, there are only people eating ice cream at the ice-cream shop," says Mimi.

"Maybe the Monkey Balloon is going down the slide!" says Mimi.

"No, there is only a little girl going down the slide," says Mimi.

"Maybe the Monkey Balloon is riding to school on the school bus!" says Mimi.

"No, there are only children riding to school on the school bus," says Mimi.

"Maybe the Monkey Balloon is swimming with fish in the ocean!" says Mimi.

"No, there are only fish swimming in the ocean," says Mimi.

"Maybe the Monkey Balloon is at the zoo!" says Mimi.

"Oh! Look, Papi! There it is!
There's the Monkey Balloon!" says Mimi.

"It looks like he found his friends," says Papi.

The End

LANGUAGE AND LEARNING TIPS

PREPOSITIONS: At twenty-four months, your child should know at least three prepositions (in, on, and under). When reading *The Monkey Balloon*, emphasize the prepositions. (For example, "The monkey is *in* the ocean.") Help your child learn prepositions with follow-up activities. Play hide-and-seek with your child, emphasizing prepositions. (For example, "I am hiding under the table," "I am hiding in the bathroom," or "I am hiding behind the couch.")

RETELLING THE STORY: Being able to recall information and sequence is an important skill in language development. In order to practice this skill, read *The Monkey Balloon* with your child, and then review the pictures and discuss what happened in the story. In the beginning you may have to prompt your child to remember the story; however, as the book becomes more familiar, your child should be able to recall where the Monkey Balloon might have gone. You can help your child by offering clues. (For example, "Maybe the monkey was riding on the _____.")

VISUAL AWARENESS: Being able to identify and locate specific items within a field of vision is an important skill for a child to develop. In order to support this visual awareness, it is important to identify, label, and comment on a specific picture within a scene when reading to your child. In *The Monkey Balloon*, encourage your child to find the Monkey Balloon on each page. When reading the book for the first time, point at the Monkey Balloon and say, "I see a Monkey Balloon." The next time you read the book, ask your child to find the balloon. Eventually, he or she should initiate the search for the Monkey Balloon. As the child develops visual awareness, ask your child to find other pictures within the scene. For example, have your child point out the stop sign on the school bus. Use this technique when reading other books with your child.

EXPANDING VOCABULARY: Expanding our vocabulary is something we all work on, even as adults. The repetitive phrases and words used in *The Monkey Balloon* help facilitate language and will help your child learn specific words. When reading the book, point out new words that your child might not know, such as "school bus" or "ocean." Depending on where you live, different words will be more familiar to your child than others. Work on expanding your child's vocabulary by consistently pointing out and identifying new things within their environment. Soon he or she will start to ask, "What is that?"

ACTIONS/VERBS: By the time your child is around fifteen-months old, he or she should be using basic action words, such as "go" and "open." When reading *The Monkey Balloon*, emphasize the actions that the Monkey Balloon is performing; for example, the Monkey Balloon is *swimming*. Then review with your child by asking, "What is the Monkey Balloon doing?" If this is too challenging for your child, prompt your child by saying,

"The Monkey Balloon is _____ ." If this is still too challenging, simply continue telling your child what actions the Monkey Balloon is performing until he or she is able to answer your questions.

While reading a story, it is important to involve your child and encourage participation in acting out what the characters are doing. This will keep your child's attention and motivates him or her to be a part of the storytelling process. For example, when the Monkey Balloon is eating ice-cream, ask your child to pretend to eat. When the Monkey Balloon is swimming, ask your child to pretend to swim. If an action is too hard for your child to act out, model it for them.

SOUNDS: Sounds are a fun way to bring a story to life! Using sounds to illustrate a story you are reading to your child encourages language development and increases the child's attention and participation. While reading *The Monkey Balloon*, think of ways to add sound effects to each page of the story. When the Monkey Balloon is on top of the ice-cream shop, you could say, "Yum! Yum!" When the balloon is going down the slide you could say "Wheeeee!" Be creative. There are no right or wrong sounds. Encourage your child to imitate you and create new sounds to illustrate the story!

PRELITERACY SKILLS: Getting your child ready to read on his or her own is very important. One of the first steps you can take to prepare your child for reading is to make him or her aware of "concepts about print." "Concepts about print" refers to the differences between words and letters and an understanding of the function of punctuation and directionality. Understanding these concepts begins when you simply ask your child to show you the front of the book, the back of the book, and the spine of the book. You should also ask your child to point to the pictures on the page and then the words on the page, ensuring that he or she understands the difference between the two. Finally, ask him or her to use a finger to show you which way we read the words on the page, ensuring that he or she understands that we read from left to right (directionality).

EXTENDED ACTIVITIES: Providing early readers with activities to go along with a story is a terrific way to keep them engaged and adds even more meaning to the reading experience. After reading *The Monkey Balloon*, it may be fun to buy your child a helium balloon. After he or she enjoys playing with the balloon, allow your child to let the balloon go, and talk with him or her about where it might end up. Have your child draw pictures of his or her balloon and where it went. Encourage your child to tell you stories about the drawings, and write the words under his or her pictures, creating your own *Monkey Balloon* story.

ABOUT THE AUTHORS:

REBECCA EISENBERG, MS, CCC-SLP, *is a certified speech-language pathologist, author, instructor, and a parent of two young children. She has multiple games and a workbook published by Super Duper Publications. She has enjoyed working with children ages 2 and up with multiple disabilities in a variety of settings for the past fourteen years.*

Rebecca has always loved and treasured children's books. Her favorite books growing up included Curious George, Corduroy, The Giving Tree and The Frog and Toad collection. She is passionate about using children's books to facilitate language and teach children valuable lessons. Rebecca began her blog, www.gravitybread.com to create a resource for parents to help make mealtime an enriched learning experience.

Rebecca lives in Armonk, NY with her husband, two children and basset hound. She can be reached at becca@gravitybread.com.

MINDY WINEBRENNER, MEd, *is an early childhood special educator, author, family-coach, and a parent of two young boys. As a child, her dream was to become a children's author and illustrator. Mindy has enjoyed working in and out of the classroom with young children and has been an advocate in promoting inclusion. While teaching in an inclusive pre-school classroom, Mindy has been able to develop her own stories, as well as adapt current children's books in order to meet the needs of her students. Currently, Mindy works with young children and their families, ages birth to five, with developmental disabilities.*

Mindy lives with her husband, two sons and Chihuahuas in Ellicott City, Maryland.

ABOUT THE ILLUSTRATOR:

YUKI OSADA *began drawing from an early age inspired by Japanese anime and manga. She is attracted to the bold use of colors and shapes such as German Expressionism and the Wiener Werkstatte (Vienna Workshop), two art movements that inspire her to create. Yuki received her BFA in illustration and digital animation from Parsons School of Design in New York City and furthered her studies at the Passalaqua School for Professional Artists (now, The Dalvero Academy) in Brooklyn, New York. Yuki's illustrations often focus on storytelling and power of narration through visual elements.*

After working as an illustration agent and freelance illustrator, Yuki began using her illustration and design skills in the apparel, paper goods and home furnishing industries. Her work as a print designer has been sold at Target, Wal-Mart, Sears/Kmart and other nationwide retailers.

Yuki currently works as a freelance textile designer and graphic artist. She spends her time creating prints and enjoys silkscreening at her home in Clearwater, Florida.

Made in the USA
Charleston, SC
29 October 2014